Is There a Ghost in the House?

"OK, who's playing tricks?" Lila demanded, after a soft thump sounded from above their heads in the dimly lit hallway.

"Wasn't that another special effect?" Jessica asked.

"I told you, there aren't any special effects up here," Lila said in a quaking voice. She started backing up.

Elizabeth gulped. If Laura Hathway really was haunting the mansion . . .

BUMP! THUMP! came the noise again.

And then everyone heard a voice. *"Ahhh-ohhh!"*

Everyone in the group screamed at the same time, and raced for the staircase.

Bantam Skylark Books in the
  SWEET VALLEY KIDS series
Ask your bookseller for the
  books you have missed

SWEET VALLEY KIDS

LILA'S HAUNTED HOUSE PARTY

Written by
Molly Mia Stewart

Created by
FRANCINE PASCAL

Illustrated by
Ying-Hwa Hu

A BANTAM SKYLARK BOOK®
NEW YORK · TORONTO · LONDON · SYDNEY · AUCKLAND

RL 2, 005–008

LILA'S HAUNTED HOUSE PARTY
A Bantam Skylark Book / October 1991

*Sweet Valley High™ and Sweet Valley Kids are
trademarks of Francine Pascal*

Conceived by Francine Pascal

*Produced by Daniel Weiss Associates, Inc.
33 West 17th Street
New York, NY 10011*

Cover art by Susan Tang
*Syklark Books is a registered trademark of Bantam Books,
a division of Bantam Doubleday Dell Publishing Group, Inc.
Registered in U.S. Patent and Trademark Office and elsewere.*

ISBN 0-553-15919-4

Published simultaneously in the United States and Canada

---

*Bantam Books are published by Bantam Books, a division of
Bantam Doubleday Dell Publishing Group, Inc. Its trademark,
consisting of the words "Bantam Books" and the portrayal of a
rooster, is Registered in U.S. Patent and Trademark Office and in
other countries. Marca Registrada. Bantam Books, 666 Fifth
Avenue, New York, New York 10103.*

PRINTED IN THE UNITED-STATES OF AMERICA

OPM   0 9 8 7 6 5 4 3 2 1

To Zachary Rosenow

CHAPTER 1

Halloween Time

"You got me!" Elizabeth Wakefield said as she grabbed her stomach and fell back on the grass. "Now *I* get to chase you and Winston with the laser beam."

Todd handed her a green Day-Glo stick. They were playing tag and pretending that the person who was "it" came from outer space.

"Watch out," Elizabeth yelled as she jumped up. "When my laser beam touches you, your skin will turn green." She chased Todd and Winston past the swings.

"Hey, Liz!" Jessica called out. "Come over here."

Elizabeth stopped running and walked over to the swings where her twin sister was talking with Lila Fowler and Eva Simpson. Many of their friends from Sweet Valley Elementary School were at the park that afternoon.

"We're talking about our Halloween costumes for the party tonight," Jessica said. "Eva is going as a turtle."

"Great idea!" Elizabeth exclaimed.

"Tell her what you're going to be," Jessica said.

Elizabeth held up her hands and curled her fingers into claws. Then she growled at Eva and Lila. "Tigerrrrrr!"

"She wanted to be a headless horseman,"

Jessica told the others. "But I said it was too creepy. I'm going to be a genie."

Elizabeth and Jessica were identical twins, but that didn't mean they always liked the same things. Elizabeth enjoyed playing outside. She was proud to be part of the Sweet Valley Soccer League. She also loved to read books, especially animal stories, and she always did her homework.

Jessica was just the opposite. She loved to play with dolls and stuffed animals. She hated getting her clothes dirty, so she didn't play sports very much. At school, she enjoyed talking with her friends more than she liked her classes. Both girls had blue-green eyes and long blond hair with bangs. Each twin wore a name bracelet, which made it easier to tell them apart.

Despite their differences, Elizabeth and Jessica loved being twins. They shared a bedroom, they shared clothes, and they could often read each other's thoughts. They were best friends.

Halloween was going to be special. Lila's father was renting a large house called Hathway Manor, and Lila had invited her entire second-grade class there for a Halloween party.

"Are you still scared because the house is supposed to be haunted?" Jessica asked Lila.

Lila frowned. Everyone in Sweet Valley had heard the rumors about Hathway Manor. People said that a ghost haunted the house. "I'm not afraid anymore," Lila said quietly. "There's no such thing as a ghost."

"Well, I believe in ghosts," Eva said.

4

"People say this one is a woman. Wouldn't it be fun if we got to see her?"

"Lila's right. There's no such thing as a ghost," Elizabeth said, laughing.

"That's right," Lila agreed, in a firmer voice this time. "There's no such thing as a ghost."

"What's the matter, Lila?" Charlie Cashman teased as he walked by. "Are you going to stay away from your own party because a ghost might get you?"

"Be quiet, Charlie," Lila shouted. "I'm not afraid of anything."

Elizabeth was surprised at how upset Lila sounded. Was Lila really still worried about ghosts?

Charlie ran away to join some of the other boys, and Elizabeth sat on one of the swings next to Eva. "Do you really think there's a ghost at Hathway Manor?" she asked.

"I don't know," Eva said, starting to swing. "But I think it's fun to believe that there might be one."

"Well, there isn't" Lila said. "My father would never give a party in a place where there was a real ghost."

"Look, everyone," Jessica shouted, as she pointed to the playing field.

The girls turned around and saw Charlie, Jerry McAllister, Ken Matthews, and Todd Wilkins walking toward them. Their arms were outstretched, and their steps were slow and clumsy. The boys were staring straight ahead and making moaning sounds.

"They're pretending to be zombies!" Elizabeth said and laughed.

"Stop it!" Lila shouted.

The boys walked closer and closer. Then all at once they started laughing. "Lila, your face is turning green," Jerry said, slapping his knee. "Did the laser beam get you, or is it the ghost? O-o-oh!"

Elizabeth laughed, too. She loved Halloween!

CHAPTER 2

The Tiger and the Genie

"Lila's party is going to be the best ever!" Jessica said at dinner that evening. "There are going to be tons of spooky special effects and a storyteller and a haunted dungeon."

"It does sound like fun," said Mrs. Wakefield.

"Yes, it does," added Mr. Wakefield. "It was nice of Lila's parents to invite all of her classmates. You'll have a great time." He waved his tie in the air, so the jack-o'-lanterns on it seemed to move. It made Jessica and Elizabeth laugh.

"Did you know that Lila's mother is related to the Hathway family?" Mr. Wakefield asked everyone. "Of course, there aren't any Hathways left now. That's why the house has been turned into a museum and is rented out for parties."

Steven, the twins' older brother, leaned across the table. "That's because no one would want to live there," he said. "Hathway Manor is haunted."

"That's just a story," Jessica said.

"Besides, ghosts aren't real," Elizabeth pointed out.

Steven shrugged. "Maybe they are, maybe they aren't. But lots of people say they've seen the ghost of a woman in the house."

"That's right," Mr. Wakefield said. "I thought I saw her once, when I was a little boy."

10

"I wonder if the ghost is looking for someone," Steven said. "Maybe she's looking for someone to be a ghost with her."

Jessica felt a shiver go up her back. She looked nervously at Elizabeth.

"I wonder, Jessica," Steven said, "if there is a ghost, how will you tell if it's real or just a special effect?"

Another shiver went up Jessica's back.

"That's enough, Steven," Mrs. Wakefield said. "Don't scare the girls out of going to the party."

"Nothing can scare me," Elizabeth said confidently. "I don't believe in ghosts anyway, no matter what Steven says."

"I don't either," Jessica agreed.

"Good," Mr. Wakefield said. "I'm sure there'll be plenty of ghosts at the party. And I'm sure they'll *all* be special effects."

"Can we get ready to go now?" Elizabeth asked, holding up her empty plate. "I'm finished."

Jessica quickly ate her last carrot. "Me, too."

"OK," their mother said with a smile. "Go put your costumes on. I'll be up in a few minutes to help you with the finishing touches."

"Great!" Jessica grabbed Elizabeth's hand, and they both ran up to their room.

Their Halloween costumes were on their beds. Jessica's genie costume was yellow and had lots of sequins sewn on it. She held it up in front of herself and looked in the mirror. "Isn't it pretty?" she said. "I love the way it sparkles."

Elizabeth was putting on her orange-and-black tiger suit. "Grrrroooowl!" she said.

12

"Did you know that Lila's mother was related to the Hathways?" Jessica asked.

"No," Elizabeth said, swinging her tiger tail back and forth.

Jessica paused for a moment. "That means that Lila's related to the ghost," she said.

"There isn't a ghost, silly," Elizabeth said.

"Well, if there *were* a ghost, Lila would be related to it," Jessica said.

"I guess you're right," Elizabeth said slowly. Then she shook her head. "But there *isn't* a ghost."

"I know," Jessica said.

Elizabeth jumped onto her bed on her hands and knees and let out another fierce growl. "And if there is, I'll bite it if it tries to get you, Jess. Don't worry."

Jessica giggled. Elizabeth looked more funny than frightening.

She was glad Elizabeth was going to be with her. She always felt safe when they were together. If there really was a ghost at Hathway Manor, it wasn't going to get them both!

"Mom has to draw whiskers on my face," Elizabeth said. "Then we'll be ready to go. I can't wait."

"Me neither," Jessica agreed.

Ghost or no ghost, Lila's Halloween party was going to be fantastic.

CHAPTER 3

The Legend of the Ghost

Mr. and Mrs. Wakefield dropped Steven off at a party at a friend's house, and then they drove the twins to Hathway Manor.

Elizabeth and Jessica walked up the long, stone path to the house. Jack-o'-lanterns with scary faces lined both sides of the path. Tall trees surrounded the old house, making it look scary. But lights shone through the windows downstairs, and Elizabeth could hear music and laughter coming from inside.

There was a sign on the door that read "Enter—If You Dare!"

"Are you ready?" Elizabeth whispered when they reached the front door.

Jessica took a deep breath and nodded. "Here we go."

Together, they pushed open the heavy, wooden door. The moment they walked in, a skeleton dropped down on them.

"AAAHHH!" Jessica screamed.

A burst of laughter echoed through the hallway. Several of their friends from Mrs. Otis's second-grade class were standing near the door.

"Were you scared?" Todd asked through his astronaut helmet. "That happens automatically when the door opens."

Elizabeth's heart was pounding, but she

smiled. "It sure was a surprise," she admitted.

"I thought the house was falling down," Jessica gasped.

"Jessica! Elizabeth!" Lila ran into the hallway. "You're here!"

Jessica's eyes opened wide. "I love your costume, Lila."

Lila was wearing a long old-fashioned frilly dress and high-buttoned boots. She was carrying a lace parasol and around her neck was a beautiful locket on the end of a chain.

"This is an antique gold locket. My father said I could wear it." Lila sounded very proud of herself.

"It's nice," Jessica said.

Elizabeth was looking around the foyer of the mansion. There were fake cobwebs hanging from the high ceiling and real candles in

18

fancy candelabras on all the tables. "This is cool," she said.

"I've already seen a lot of the special effects," Lila boasted. "They're not as scary as I thought they would be."

Just then, a ghostly man wrapped in chains sprung out of a trap door in one of the floorboards. Lila screamed and dropped her parasol.

"I thought you weren't scared of anything!" Ken said through howls of laughter.

Lila picked up her parasol and scowled at Ken. "Come on, everyone," she said. "There's a storyteller in the ballroom. He's going to start soon."

Elizabeth followed the others toward a large doorway. As she passed a wide staircase, she stopped and stared at a painting hanging in the stairwell.

"Hey, Lila. Jessica. Look," she said.

They stopped and looked where she was pointing. The painting was a portrait of a young woman in old-fashioned clothes. She had light brown hair and green eyes.

"She looks just like you, Lila," Jessica gasped.

Lila's face turned pink. "She does not. Come on, we're going to be late for the story-teller."

The girls went into the ballroom, where tall candles made dancing shadows on the walls.

"Welcome to Hathway Manor," said an old man in a rocking chair. He rocked back and forth a few times without saying anything else.

Elizabeth sat on the floor next to Jessica. She loved hearing storytellers. It was like listening to someone read a book out loud, only better.

"You've probably all heard rumors about this house," the storyteller began. "Let me tell you right from the start—they're true!"

A startled gasp came from the crowd.

"Laura Hathway was an invalid," he went on softly. "She could hardly take three steps from her wheelchair without growing faint. Her older brother Michael was devoted to her, though. He helped her all the time and took care of her."

Elizabeth's heart was beginning to beat faster. She took Jessica's hand and squeezed it.

"Then the Hathways fell on hard times, and Michael decided to try his fortune way up in the Yukon gold territories," the storyteller said. "Laura became very sick while he

21

was away. In her sleep she cried out 'Come back! Come back!'"

The storyteller leaned forward in his rocking chair. "But he didn't come back. Laura died, and now she wanders the house, still searching for her brother."

"Have you ever seen her?" Amy Sutton asked.

"Yes, many times," he answered. "She holds out her hands and asks for help. You can see her portrait out in the hall, by the stairs."

Lila clapped both hands over her mouth. Her eyes were wide, and she looked scared. Elizabeth guessed Lila *did* think she looked like Laura.

"'Come back! Come back,'" the storyteller moaned.

Some of the boys and girls screamed, but

they all looked like they were having fun.

"Remember, Laura's bedroom was on the second floor," the storyteller warned them in a hoarse whisper. "So don't go up there unless you want Laura to—*get you!*"

CHAPTER 4

The Portrait

"That story was really scary," Jessica said to Lila, as they walked out of the ballroom.

"I wasn't scared," Lila said, but her voice was a little shaky.

"A-a-a-a-a-ahhhhh!!!!" Someone in a Dracula costume jumped out at them with a bloodcurdling yell. He had false fangs in his mouth and fake blood running down his face. Lila grabbed Jessica's arm and screamed.

"Ha, ha, got you!" Charlie Cashman yelled, grinning at them.

"That's not funny," Lila said.

"I thought you weren't going to be scared," Charlie said.

Lila frowned angrily. "I wasn't scared. You just surprised me, that's all."

"Lila!" Todd called from the hallway. "Look at the painting of Laura Hathway. She looks just like you."

"See?" Jessica said. "They think so, too."

"She does not," Lila insisted, folding her arms. "She doesn't look anything like me at all."

"Why don't you stand next to the painting," Elizabeth suggested. "That way we can compare."

"No." Lila shook her head.

Charlie and Jerry started to laugh. "Why not? Are you afraid you'll turn into a ghost?"

Charlie asked. "Go stand next to it, Lila. I mean, *Laura*. I dare you!"

"No!" Lila shouted.

"Do you think Laura will get you if you do?" Todd asked her in a deep, ghostly voice.

"Laura wants a friend, Lila," Jerry said. "She's calling to you!"

"Aaaah!" Charlie screamed again. "Be my ghost friend, Lila."

Jessica wanted to laugh at the way the boys were acting. But she could see that Lila didn't think they were funny.

The boys ran off into one of the other rooms. Elizabeth was talking to Amy and Todd, and Jessica was left standing alone with Lila in the hallway.

Jessica looked up the wide staircase. It was so dark she could barely see the top

steps. She wondered what might be up there. "Hey, Lila," she whispered. "Do you want to go upstairs?"

Lila started twirling her parasol nervously. "The party is only on this floor and in the basement," she said. "There's nothing to see up there."

"I know," Jessica said. She was secretly happy that Lila didn't want to go upstairs to the second floor. But she was also beginning to get very curious about the ghost.

CHAPTER 5

The Creepy Dungeon

"This way to the haunted dungeon," cackled a woman dressed as a witch. She narrowed her eyes and, with one of her long, crooked fingers, beckoned to Elizabeth, Jessica, and Lila. She pointed to the cellar door. "Be careful, my pretties, or you'll never come out."

Jessica gulped. "It's just pretend," she whispered to the others.

"She's right. There's nothing to be scared of," Elizabeth said. They both looked at Lila.

"My dad told me what to expect," Lila said confidently. "I'll lead the way."

The three girls walked through the keyhole-shaped door and down the dark, wooden stairs.

When they were halfway down, they heard a low, ghostly moan coming through the walls. Elizabeth grabbed the banister, then let go quickly. "Yuck," she said. "My hand's covered with gooey slime."

"So is mine," Jessica said. "Look at those lights." Jessica pointed ahead to some flashing lights that surrounded a sign. "WARNING! NO RETURN!" it said.

"I guess we have to crawl through here," Elizabeth whispered. She kneeled down in front of a small, round opening and peeked in. "I can't see anything!" she said.

Lila laughed nervously. "Oh, go on. Don't be scared."

"I'm not scared," Elizabeth announced. "I'm going in!"

Elizabeth crawled through the opening into a tunnel. She could feel threads brush by her face. They felt like cobwebs. *It's just pretend*, she reminded herself. Jessica and Lila were following close behind. Once, Jessica accidentally knelt on Elizabeth's tiger tail, and both of them were so surprised that they screamed.

The tunnel became very narrow and suddenly slanted downward. Then the walls started shaking! The girls could hear screaming and wailing. Elizabeth jumped nervously, but then she laughed. Through a tiny window she saw a man chained to the dungeon wall. He rattled the chains and

32

begged for water. Through another window, she saw three witches stirring a bubbling caldron.

"Would one of you girls like to help us stir?" asked one of the witches. There was a big wart on her nose, and her laugh was a high-pitched cackle.

"They're gross!" Lila said.

"Let's hurry," Jessica told Elizabeth.

Elizabeth nodded and crawled more quickly.

Soon they found themselves in a dark passageway where they could finally stand up. Elizabeth looked around. Something flew above her. Flapping wings grazed her head. "Are those bats?" she asked, ducking.

"I don't know," Jessica answered, "but they sound like bats."

Lila didn't say anything. She just grabbed

Elizabeth's and Jessica's hands, and the three of them ran to the exit door. It opened to show a set of stairs leading up to the backyard.

"Phew!" Elizabeth said as she reached the top.

"That was pretty scary," Lila said, dusting off her old-fashioned dress.

"This way to the haunted graveyard," Jessica said. She could see a group of kids ahead of them, running between large headstones.

"Is this a real graveyard?" Elizabeth asked Lila. "Do you think Laura Hathway is buried here?"

Lila shook her head. "I don't know," she said. "I *think* it's all fake."

"Well, it's a lot of fun," Elizabeth said. She stopped and looked back at the Hathway mansion. When she glanced up at the third floor, she saw a soft, flickering light in one of the windows. It looked like someone holding a candle.

"Look," she said, catching up to Jessica and Lila. "There're more special effects in the attic."

"The party is only on the first floor and the basement," Lila reminded her. "There's nothing upstairs."

Elizabeth, Jessica, and Lila looked up at the third-floor windows. There was no light flickering anymore. But now they were all thinking about the ghost of Laura Hathway again.

"There isn't *supposed* to be anything up there," Lila said in a worried voice.

Elizabeth could tell that Lila was getting very nervous. "It was probably just my imagination," she said.

"You're always imagining things," Jessica said.

"I guess so," Lila said. She looked at Elizabeth. "You just *thought* you saw something, right?"

Very slowly, Elizabeth nodded. Deep down inside, though, she knew she really had seen a light in the window.

Was it the ghost of Laura Hathway?

CHAPTER 6

The Creaking Steps

Jessica led the way back into the mansion. "Let's see if they've started the Halloween games," she said.

In the ballroom, some of the kids were bobbing for apples, while others were playing pin-the-tail-on-the-black-cat. Near the food table, some of the boys were holding strange-looking things.

"What's that?" Elizabeth asked, walking over to them.

"Watch!" Ken said. He picked up a piece of candy from a tray. It looked just like an eyeball. Ken popped it into his mouth. "Mmm, good!" he said.

"That's disgusting!" Jessica said with a shiver. "I'm not eating any of those!"

"What does it taste like?" Elizabeth wanted to know.

Todd popped one into his mouth. "It tastes like an eyeball!" he yelled. He ate another one.

Grinning, Elizabeth took one and put it into her mouth and chewed. "It's good," she told Jessica and Lila. "I think they're made out of sugar."

"You go first," Lila giggled.

Jessica picked one up.

"Look out, it blinked," Winston Egbert warned.

"Yuck!" Jessica dropped it like a hot potato, and everyone laughed.

On another tray were crackers shaped like fingers. Jessica tried one. It was very crunchy.

"This is the coolest party, Lila," Ken said happily.

Todd looked around. "Has anyone seen Charlie or Jerry?"

Nobody answered.

"They were here a little while ago," Winston said.

Ken crunched on a finger cracker. "The last time I saw them they were standing at the bottom of the staircase."

Jessica swallowed the eyeball she had taken without biting into it. "The stairs to the second floor?" she asked.

Everyone standing around the table was silent. Jessica looked from face to face. Were they thinking about the ghost, just like she was?

Elizabeth shrugged. "Those two are always going off by themselves."

"They wouldn't go upstairs, would they?" Lila asked.

Todd fidgeted with his costume. "They said they wanted to see if . . ." he mumbled.

"See if what?" Jessica asked nervously.

"They should have come back by now," Winston added.

No one said anything for a moment.

"Well, I'm not going up there to look for them!" Lila said.

The boys all began to smile.

"Why not?" Ken asked.

"It's your party, Lila," Todd pointed out. "*You* should look for them."

Jessica watched to see what Lila would do. She was feeling worried, herself.

"We can all go," Elizabeth said. "If we go in a group, it won't be so scary."

"I'm not scared," Todd said bravely.

"Then *you* go!" Lila told him angrily. "Show us just how brave you are!"

Elizabeth gave Lila an encouraging smile. "Come on. We can all go together."

"You're not scared, Jessica, are you?" Winston asked in a teasing voice.

Jessica gulped. "No," she said, but she didn't feel very brave.

"And Elizabeth isn't scared," Winston said. "Come on, Lila. You don't want to miss the fun, do you?"

Lila started fiddling with the locket around her neck. She twirled it between her fingers and zipped it back and forth along the chain. She didn't answer Winston.

"Are you ready?" Ken asked her with a big smile.

"I'll bet they're not even up there," Lila said, hoping everyone would decide not to go.

"We should still look for them," Elizabeth said. "The sooner we look upstairs, the sooner we can come back down."

Jessica wished her sister wouldn't act so brave all the time. She didn't want to go upstairs at all anymore. What if Laura's ghost trapped them in one of the rooms? She didn't want the others to think she was afraid, though, so she followed Elizabeth.

When they reached the bottom of the staircase, everyone made room for Lila, so she could go first. The stairs went up and up to a dark landing, and then they turned a corner.

"Hurry," Ken said.

Lila took a deep breath, and put her foot on the first creaking step. "OK," she whispered. "I'm going."

CHAPTER 7

Strange Noises

One by one, each person tiptoed up the staircase. The steps creaked under their feet.

"There's a light on," Ken said in a hushed voice, as they stopped on the landing and looked up at the top.

"Let's keep going," Elizabeth said.

"What was that?" Jessica whispered.

Everyone stopped to listen.

"I didn't hear anything," Todd said, sounding worried.

"Me neither," Elizabeth said. Her heart

was going *bumpety-bump* inside her chest. She knew there was no such thing as a real ghost, but she was sure she had seen a flickering light in the upstairs window. It hadn't been her imagination. *So what—or who—was it?* she wondered nervously.

There were a few bare light bulbs in the hallway, but they only made it seem more gloomy. The floor was covered with a layer of dust, and the hall smelled dirty and stuffy. The doors on both sides were shut.

Lila's eyes were wide. She stopped short and didn't budge.

"Come on," Jessica said, tugging on Lila's sleeve. "We can't just stay here."

"OK, OK," Lila whispered.

Elizabeth took a deep breath and crossed the hall to the first door.

"Don't open it!" Jessica begged.

47

Elizabeth tried to turn the doorknob. It didn't move. "It's locked," she told the others.

The boys looked embarrassed that Elizabeth had gone first. Todd and Ken and Winston each walked to a door and tried the knobs.

"They're all locked," Todd said, sounding relieved.

"Maybe Charlie and Jerry didn't come up here, after all," Lila said hopefully. She turned and headed for the stairs.

"Lila! You can't leave yet!" Jessica said. "We just started looking."

Lila stopped and frowned.

"Maybe they did come up," Winston suggested. "And Laura Hathway got them."

With a squeak of fright, Lila ran across the hall to stand next to Jessica. They both looked around with wide eyes.

48

Elizabeth walked down the hallway, trying each of the doors. The others followed her, their footsteps echoing loudly.

"I give up," Todd said just as a soft thump sounded from over their heads. Elizabeth froze and stared up at the ceiling. Everyone else stopped behind her.

"OK, who's playing tricks?" Lila demanded. "Winston, I know it was you."

Winston's mouth dropped open in surprise. "It was not!"

"Wasn't that another special effect?" Jessica asked. She took a step closer to Elizabeth.

"I told you, there aren't any special effects up here," Lila said in a quaking voice. She started backing up. "And everything's locked . . ."

Elizabeth gulped. She felt like someone

was running a finger up her spine. If Laura Hathway really was haunting the mansion . . .

BUMP! THUMP! came the noise again.

Then everyone heard a voice. *"Ahhh-ohhh!"*

Everyone in the group screamed at the same time, then turned and raced for the staircase.

CHAPTER 8

Lila's Locket

Jessica and the others didn't stop running until they reached the front door. Jessica was about to pull it open and run outside, but Elizabeth stopped her.

"I'm getting out of here!" Jessica insisted.

"No, wait," Elizabeth said.

Todd, Ken, Winston, and Lila were all standing by the door, too. "Do you think the ghost got Charlie and Jerry?" Winston asked.

Nobody answered. Jessica was sure that the answer was yes.

"This is going to ruin the party," Lila complained.

"Do you think we should tell Lila's father or any of the other grown-ups?" Elizabeth asked.

Todd looked embarrassed. "Let's not tell them we ran away," he said softly.

"I don't want to tell anyone what happened at all!" Lila said, sounding very upset. "I'll get all the blame."

Elizabeth glanced over at the staircase. "Maybe . . ." she began.

Jessica guessed right away what Elizabeth was thinking. The twins could often read each other's thoughts.

"No way," Jessica said, shaking her head and reaching for the doorknob.

"I think maybe we should go back up and look for them again," Elizabeth said finally.

"I'm not going back," Lila said firmly. "No way."

"Me neither," Winston said. "If the ghost has them, it's too late."

Jessica looked at Lila. Lila looked scared. Suddenly, Jessica looked closely at Lila's neck.

"Hey, Lila," she said. "Where's your locket?"

"My locket?" Lila looked down and let out a gasp. "It's gone! Oh, no! Now I'll really be in trouble!"

"Why?" Elizabeth asked.

Lila was starting to cry. "I wasn't really supposed to wear it," she said. "But I kept asking and asking my dad until he finally said yes. I promised him I'd be very careful with it, because the thing that fastens it was a little bit loose!" She burst into tears.

"Where did you lose it?" Elizabeth asked. "Do you remember?"

Lila wiped her eyes. "I had it before . . . when we were up *there*," she finished in a frightened whisper.

"You lost your necklace upstairs?" Jessica asked. "Oh, no!"

"You have to help me find it," Lila said, grabbing Jessica's hand. "Please, please? Pretty please with sugar on top?"

Jessica bit her lip. "Now you want to go back upstairs?" she asked. "Where the ghost is?"

"Please!" Lila repeated. She started to cry again. "You have to help me find my locket."

Jessica looked at the others. Ken, Todd, and Winston looked at the floor.

"I'm not going," Ken said. He hurried to join some of his friends in the other room.

"I'm not either," Winston said, following Ken.

"I don't see what's so important about an old necklace," Todd said. He started backing up. "I'm going to see what Ken and Winston are doing."

Watching the boys leave, Lila let out another sob.

"I'll go with you," Elizabeth said reluctantly. "We have to look for Charlie and Jerry again, anyway."

"Oh, brother," Jessica said. "OK, Lila. I'll go, too."

CHAPTER 9

The Secret Door

Elizabeth, Jessica, and Lila linked their arms together. It gave them the courage to walk back up the wide, creaking staircase. Elizabeth looked at her sister. She could tell Jessica was very scared.

"There's nothing to be afraid of," Elizabeth said, trying to sound calm.

"How do you know?" Lila asked.

Step by step, they climbed up to the landing. "Do you hear or see anything?" Jessica whispered as they reached the second floor.

"Not yet," Elizabeth said.

Lila looked fearfully back down the stairs. "Do we have to do this?"

"You're the one who lost your necklace," Jessica pointed out. They started walking down the corridor.

"I know," Lila said. "But I—"

THUMP! BUMP! came a noise from over their heads.

Elizabeth froze. Jessica grabbed Elizabeth's tiger tail. Lila covered her eyes with both hands.

BUMPA-KABUNK! TAP TAP.

"Don't let it get me!" Lila begged with her hands still covering her eyes.

Elizabeth raised her eyes slowly to the ceiling. The noises were coming from the attic.

"You know," she whispered. "Maybe Charlie and Jerry are making those noises."

Jessica frowned. "You mean, it's not the ghost?"

Instead of answering, Elizabeth called out, "Charlie? Jerry? Are you up there?"

THUMP THUMP came the reply. Then a muffled voice came down through the ceiling.

"Eee-ah-uh-aw!"

"That's definitely a ghost!" Lila said. She started backing up toward the stairs.

"Wait a second," Elizabeth said. "That could be them trying to answer."

Lila shook her head. "That's Laura Hathway's ghost," she said. "I'm not staying here to get caught by it."

She turned around and began walking back to the staircase. But then she stopped.

"Look!" she gasped. "My locket!"

"You found it?" Jessica asked.

Lila walked to the side of the hallway and bent over. "Here it is!" she said excitedly. Then she bent down farther. "Look! There are footprints in the dust, and they look like they go right into the wall," she added. She had a puzzled look on her face. "Only a ghost could walk through a wall."

Elizabeth kneeled down to look at the footprints. "Maybe there's a secret door," she said.

"Wow!" Jessica gasped. "Wouldn't it be great if we found it?"

"There's no doorknob," Lila said.

"There wouldn't be a doorknob if it's a *secret* door," Jessica pointed out.

While Lila and Jessica talked, Elizabeth felt all over the paneling for a button or a latch. She couldn't find anything.

"I don't think it's a secret door," Lila said,

putting her necklace back on. "I think the ghost just walked through the wall."

"But ghosts don't wear sneakers," Elizabeth said. "Those are sneaker footprints."

Lila sighed. She didn't seem to be so scared anymore. "Well, I still don't think Charlie and Jerry are here. They probably just left the party early." She leaned against the paneling.

"I give up," Elizabeth said, stepping back.

Suddenly the panel swung back on a hidden hinge, and Lila toppled backward into the dark!

CHAPTER 10

The Flickering Light

Jessica was too shocked to scream. She just stared at the opening in the wall which Lila had fallen through.

"Ouch!" Lila's voice came out of the dark. "I bumped my elbow!"

"You found a secret passage!" Elizabeth shouted.

Jessica began to feel excited, too. "This is unbelievable!"

They stepped into the opening. Lila was standing up, brushing off her dress. The three girls looked around. They were in a narrow passage between the hallway and the next room. Real cobwebs hung from the ceiling.

"There's a staircase," Elizabeth whispered. "Let's see where it leads."

Jessica looked back. She could see a bare light bulb hanging in the hallway. "Let's not close the secret door," she warned. "I don't want to get stuck in here."

"Good idea," Elizabeth said. "Let's go."

Together the girls climbed up the narrow set of stairs. "I'll bet it goes to the attic," Lila whispered.

Elizabeth stopped. "I see a light," she said in a hushed voice.

Jessica peered over her sister's shoulder. Up ahead, she could see a faint glow, too. "You don't think it's the ghost, do you?" she asked.

Elizabeth shook her head. Then she took

another step up. "Who's there!" she shouted suddenly.

Jessica was so startled she almost fell down the stairs.

"It's us!" came a frightened voice.

Elizabeth, Jessica, and Lila ran up the rest of the stairs to the attic. Huddled in a corner they found Charlie and Jerry. The two class troublemakers looked tired and worried.

"We found you!" Lila said triumphantly.

Charlie picked up a weak flashlight and shone it on them. "Hey, it's Lila, Elizabeth, and Jessica," he said.

"Was that you making those noises?" Jessica asked them.

"Were you trying to scare us?" Lila demanded.

"Were you trapped?" Elizabeth asked.

The boys stood up. "Charlie closed the secret door, and we couldn't open it again. So we were stuck," Jerry explained.

"But we weren't scared," Charlie said quickly.

Jessica looked at the other girls. She had a feeling Charlie and Jerry had been terrified!

"Let's get out of here," Lila suggested. "You two almost ruined the party."

Elizabeth snapped her fingers. "Hey, it must have been your flashlight I saw when we were out in the backyard," she said. "That explains the light I saw."

"Phew," Lila said. She started to giggle. "You know, I almost believed there really was a ghost in this creepy old house."

"*Almost* believed?" Jessica said, shaking her head. "You were certain."

"Come on," Elizabeth said, waving everyone toward the stairs. "Let's go."

Once they all reached the first floor, they told their friends about the secret passageway. Charlie and Jerry bragged about finding it first, and the girls bragged about rescuing them.

"You had to be rescued by a bunch of girls," Winston teased.

"Yeah, and *you* were too chicken to go up and look for them again," Jessica snapped at Winston.

Winston's face turned red.

All the kids took turns going upstairs to look at the secret door. But it was getting late, and parents were starting to arrive. Soon, all the guests were gone except for Lila, her father, the twins, and Mr. and Mrs. Wakefield.

"Thank you for inviting everyone in Lila's

class," Mr. Wakefield told Mr. Fowler. "Elizabeth and Jessica had a great time."

"It was my pleasure," Mr. Fowler said. "I hope none of the kids were too scared."

"No way," Lila boasted. "I wasn't scared."

Jessica and Elizabeth giggled. Lila laughed, too.

"Well, it's time to go," Mrs. Wakefield said. "Come on, girls. It's getting late."

Everyone left the house at the same time and waited for Mr. Fowler to lock the front door. Jessica walked a few steps down the path with Elizabeth and Lila.

"Look at the house," Elizabeth said, turning around. "It's so spooky-looking in the moonlight."

"Sure is," Jessica agreed. She kept staring up at the dark, gloomy mansion while Elizabeth and Lila walked to the cars. Suddenly, a flickering light caught Jessica's eye.

"Look!" she gasped.

"What?" Elizabeth asked, as she turned around.

Jessica pointed to the attic windows. "I saw a light up there!" she said, sounding excited.

"It was probably just a reflection of a streetlight or the moon, Jessica," Mr. Wakefield said sensibly. "That's all."

Jessica shook her head. "I know I saw a light," she whispered.

If Charlie and Jerry weren't up there with a flashlight anymore, then . . .

Elizabeth and Lila walked back to Jessica. The three of them stared up at the mansion again. If the house was empty, and it wasn't

the moon Jessica had seen—could there be a ghost, after all?

Two days later, Jessica was still thinking about the ghost. She and Elizabeth were eating lunch in the cafeteria at school.

"I'm sure I saw a light," she insisted.

Elizabeth put her sandwich down on her tray. "*I* believe you," she said. "But maybe there's an explanation. The light I saw was just Charlie's flashlight. At least I think it was."

"Let's not talk about it anymore," Jessica said as Ellen Riteman and Lila came over to join them.

"Hi," Jessica said.

"Hi, identical twin," Ellen teased. Jessica and Elizabeth were wearing identical outfits that day, so it was even harder than usual to tell them apart.

"Maybe I'm an identical triplet," Jessica said with a mysterious smile.

"What do you mean?" Lila asked.

Jessica shrugged. "Our cousin Kelly is coming to visit us at Thanksgiving. She looks just like us. You'll see when you meet her."

"I hope Kelly will have fun," Elizabeth said. "She didn't sound very excited on the phone."

"That's true," Jessica agreed. "Maybe something is bothering her."

"Or maybe there's a secret reason why she's visiting you," Lila said in her know-it-all voice. "And if there is, I'll find out."

Is the twins' cousin hiding something? Find out in Sweet Valley Kids #24, COUSIN KELLY'S FAMILY SECRET.

SWEET VALLEY KIDS

Jessica and Elizabeth have had lots of adventures in *Sweet Valley High* and *Sweet Valley Twins*...now read about the twins at age seven! You'll love all the fun that comes with being seven—birthday parties, playing dress-up, class projects, putting on puppet shows and plays, losing a tooth, setting up lemonade stands, caring for animals and much more! It's all part of SWEET VALLEY KIDS. Read them all!

SWEET VALLEY TWINS™

Buy them at your local bookstore or use this handy page for ordering:

Bantam Books, Dept. SVT3, 414 East Golf Road, Des Plaines, IL 60016

Please send me the items I have checked above. I am enclosing $_____
(please add $2.50 to cover postage and handling). Send check or money
order, no cash or C.O.D.s please.

Mr/Ms _____

Address _____

City/State _____ Zip _____

Please allow four to six weeks for delivery.
Prices and availability subject to change without notice.